This Little Tiger book belongs to:

_____

_____

_____

For Mat, and helpful cups of tea in the early hours
— O. H.

For Linda, my creative guardian angel. Her generosity has
helped me sleep a little better at night. Thank you
— C. P.

LITTLE TIGER PRESS LTD,
an imprint of the Little Tiger Group
1 Coda Studios, 189 Munster Road, London SW6 6AW
Imported into the EEA by Penguin Random House Ireland,
Morrison Chambers, 32 Nassau Street, Dublin D02 YH68
www.littletiger.co.uk

First published in Great Britain 2017
This edition published 2020
Text by Owen Hart • Text copyright © 2017 Little Tiger Press Ltd
Illustrations copyright © 2017 Caroline Pedler
Caroline Pedler has asserted her right to be identified as the illustrator
of this work under the Copyright, Designs and Patents Act, 1988
A CIP catalogue record for this book is available from the British Library
All rights reserved

LTP/1800/4359/1121 • ISBN 978-1-78881-800-1
Manufactured, printed, and assembled in Guangdong, China
Fourth printing, November 2021
4 6 8 10 9 7 5

I Can't Sleep!

by Owen Hart   Illustrated by Caroline Pedler

LiTTLE TiGER

LONDON

It was the middle of the night.
All was quiet on board the *Leaping Salmon*.
But Mole couldn't sleep.

"Fiddlesticks!" he sighed
and padded across the
deck. He pushed open
Mouse's door.

"Mouse! Mouse!" he called. "I can't sleep. Can I come in here with you?"

Mouse yawned and peered at Mole in the moonlight. "Sure," he said. "Don't forget your blanket."

While Mole plumped
up the pillows,
Mouse had an idea.
"Let's read a bedtime story,"
he said.
"Yippee!" cheered Mole.

As Mouse turned the pages,
Mole began to feel sleepy.
But as soon as they reached
the happily ever after,
Mole cried, "It's too short!
Can we read another one?"

Mole picked a second book,
and Mouse began to read.
But then Mole gave a sudden squeak.
"Too scary!" he cried.
"This won't help me sleep!"

So Mouse read a third story,
about a boat just like theirs.
"Ahhh," sighed Mole. "That was just right."
And he settled down to sleep.

But Mole wasn't
quiet for long.
"Mouse! Mouse!"
he called.
"I still can't sleep!"

"Why not?" asked Mouse.
"It's too dark!" said Mole.
"And I can't stop thinking
about the scary story."

Mouse turned on the
lamp. A soft glow
filled the room,
and soon Mole was
silent again . . .

. . . but only for a while.
"Mouse!" he cried. "Now it's too bright!"

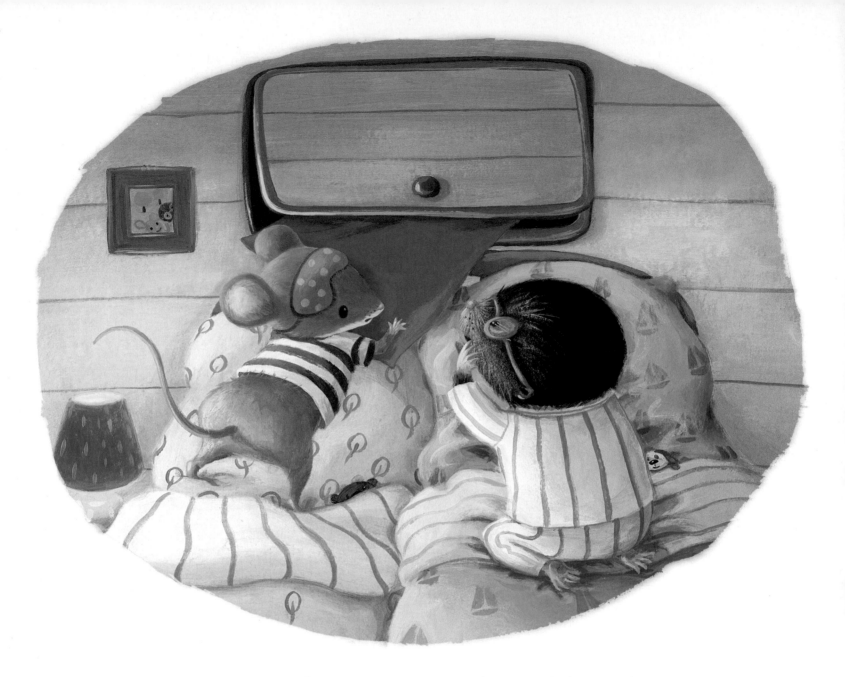

Luckily, Mouse had a better idea.
He opened the door to the cubby above
his bed and took out a large piece of paper.
"That won't help me sleep!" said Mole.
"Watch," said Mouse.

Mouse began to
cut the paper.
Mole looked on
in wonder.

With a tuck
and a fold,
Mouse had
made the
perfect
lampshade.

"Wow—look at that!" exclaimed Mole as stars and moons danced on the walls. "It's just right." And he rolled over with a happy sigh.

But Mole didn't stay still for long.
"Mouse! Mouse!" he called.
"I STILL can't sleep. I'm too cold!"

Mouse looked in
the drawer under
his bed and took out
a warm blanket.
"You can use this," he said.
Mole pulled the blanket
right up to his chin and
closed his tired eyes.

"Mouse!"
he squeaked.
"Now I'm too hot!"
"Even without the
blanket?" asked Mouse.
"Yes!" fretted Mole.

So Mouse had his
best idea of all.
"But I'll need your
help," he told Mole.
Together, they moved
the chair . . .

and dragged the
dresser . . .

and tugged at
the trunk.

With one last push, the bed was
right next to the open window.
"That's perfect," said Mole.
"Thank you, Mouse."
And he snuggled under the covers.

At last all was peaceful.
The river lapped gently.
A frog croaked softly.
And everything was quiet
aboard the *Leaping Salmon*.

But not for long . . . .

"Mole! Mole!"
called Mouse.
"I can't sleep!"

It wasn't too dark
or too light.

And it wasn't too
hot or too cold.

What could be wrong?

"Mole!" cried Mouse.
"STOP THAT SNORING!"